PUFFIN BOOKS
DIARY OF A WIMPY KID
THE LONG HAUL

BOOKS BY JEFF KINNEY

Diary of a Wimpy Kid

Diary of a Wimpy Kid: Rodrick Rules

Diary of a Wimpy Kid: The Last Straw

Diary of a Wimpy Kid: Dog Days

Diary of a Wimpy Kid: The Ugly Truth

Diary of a Wimpy Kid: Cabin Fever

Diary of a Wimpy Kid: The Third Wheel

Diary of a Wimpy Kid: Hard Luck

Diary of a Wimpy Kid: Old School

The Wimpy Kid Do-It-Yourself Book

The Wimpy Kid Movie Diary

COMING SOON

More Diary of a Wimpy Kid

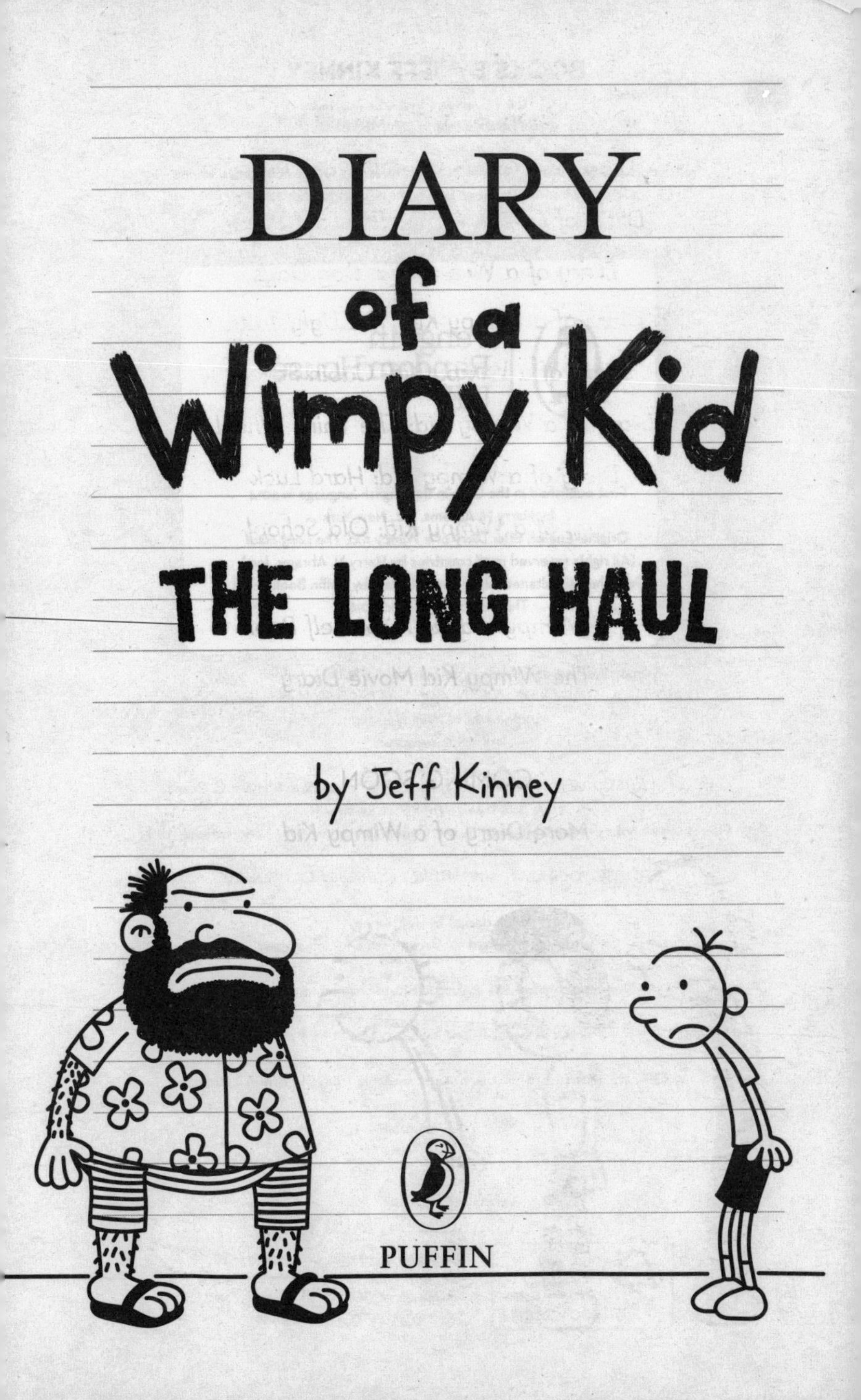
DIARY
of a
Wimpy Kid
THE LONG HAUL
by Jeff Kinney
PUFFIN

PUFFIN BOOKS

UK | USA | Canada | Ireland | Australia
India | New Zealand | South Africa

Puffin Books is part of the Penguin Random House group of companies whose addresses can be found at global.penguinrandomhouse.com.

puffinbooks.com

Book design by Jeff Kinney
Cover design by Chad W. Beckerman and Jeff Kinney

The moral right of the author/illustrator has been asserted

Printed in Great Britain by Clays Ltd, St Ives plc

A CIP catalogue record for this book is available from the British Library

ISBN: 978-0-141-35422-4

www.greenpenguin.co.uk

Penguin Random House is committed to a sustainable future for our business, our readers and our planet. This book is made from Forest Stewardship Council® certified paper.

TO PRANAV

JUNE

Friday

If there's one thing I've learned from my years of being a kid, it's that you have ZERO control over your own life.

Ever since school let out, I haven't had anything I've needed to DO or anywhere I've needed to BE. As long as the air-conditioning was working and the TV remote had batteries in it, I was all set for a relaxing summer holiday.

But then, out of the blue, THIS happened –

This isn't the FIRST time Mom has sprung a trip on us without any warning. Last year on the first day of summer, she said we were going upstate for a few days to visit Aunt Loretta at the nursing home.

It wasn't exactly my idea of a fun way to kick off the summer. One time when we visited Aunt Loretta, her roommate grabbed me and wouldn't let go until a staffer gave her a chocolate-chip muffin.

But Mom was just bluffing about going to the nursing home. At breakfast the next morning, she told us where we were REALLY going.

Me and my brother Rodrick were happy, because we were both dreading spending the first week of our summer holiday playing shuffleboard at a nursing home.

But when my little brother, Manny, heard about the change in plans he totally LOST it. Mom had talked up the Aunt Loretta trip so much that Manny was actually EXCITED about going.

We ended up POSTPONING our trip to Disney so we could visit Aunt Loretta. You'd think Mom would've learned her lesson about surprise trips after THAT one.

I know EXACTLY where this road-trip idea came from, because the new issue of "Family Frolic" magazine came in the mail today.

If I had to guess, I'd say 90% of everything we do as a family comes from ideas Mom gets from that magazine. And when I saw the latest issue I knew it was gonna get Mom's wheels turning.

I've flipped through "Family Frolic" a few times, and I have to admit the pictures always make everything look like a lot of fun.

But there must be something wrong with OUR family, because we can never measure up to the ones they show in the magazine.

I guess Mom's not giving up, though. She said this road trip is gonna be awesome and that spending a lot of time together in the car will be a "bonding" experience for the whole family.

I tried to talk her into letting us do something NORMAL, like going to a water park for the day, but Mom didn't want to hear it.

She said the whole point of this trip is to do things we've never done before and to have "authentic" experiences.

I thought Mom would've looped Dad in about her road-trip idea, but apparently I was wrong. Because when he got home from work he seemed just as surprised as us kids.

Dad told Mom it was a bad time to be away from work and he didn't want to use his vacation days unless he absolutely HAD to. But Mom said there's nothing more important than spending time with your family.

Then Dad told Mom he was really hoping to get his BOAT out on the water this weekend, and if we went on a road trip he wouldn't be able to.

Mom and Dad get along pretty well in general, but the one thing that's guaranteed to cause a fight between them is Dad's boat.

A few years ago, Mom sent Dad out to get some milk, but along the way he spotted a boat for sale in someone's front yard. And, before you knew it, the boat was in our driveway.

Mom was mad that Dad didn't check with her first, because having a boat is a ton of work.

But Dad said it was always his dream to own a boat and that we could spend every weekend out on the water as a family.

So Dad got to KEEP the boat, and he seemed really happy. But things went downhill fast.

A few days later, some people from the Homeowners' Association knocked on our door.

They said there were rules in our neighbourhood against having a boat parked in front of your house and told Dad he had to move it to the back.

The boat sat in the backyard for the whole summer because Dad was too busy and didn't have time to use it. Then, in the autumn, one of Dad's co-workers told him he'd have to WINTERIZE the boat to protect it from the cold weather.

Dad found out it would cost more to winterize the boat than it cost him to BUY it, so he decided he'd take his chances. And, sure enough, two weeks later, when the temperature dropped below freezing, a big crack appeared in the hull.

When it started to snow, Dad rolled the boat under the back deck, and it sat there all winter. In the spring, Mom started using it to store all sorts of junk from the house.

The next summer, Dad decided he was gonna fix the boat.

But when he went to pull it out from under the deck he discovered a family of raccoons living in our old washing machine.

Dad called an exterminator to get rid of the raccoons, but when he heard how much THAT was gonna cost he decided to take care of it himself.

By then Manny had heard about the baby raccoons living in the washing machine, and Mom had to step in.

The boat's been sitting there ever since. I haven't heard any scurrying sounds coming from under the deck for a while, so I'm guessing the raccoons moved out.

Today, Mom told Dad he had the whole rest of the summer to get his boat out on the water, and he pretty much gave up after that.

Mom said we were gonna leave first thing in the morning, so we needed to start packing for the trip. She told everyone to bring the "bare essentials" so we could fit everything in the minivan.

But by the time we got all our stuff out in the driveway it was pretty clear we had a space problem.

Mom started going through everything and sorting it into two piles - the things we needed and the things we didn't. Rodrick was pretty disappointed when some of his "essentials" didn't make the cut.

Mom made me leave a bunch of small stuff behind, which seemed pretty ridiculous considering that Manny's plastic potty was coming along for the ride.

Whenever we take a trip that's longer than fifteen minutes, Mom brings Manny's potty "just in case". But I get really uncomfortable whenever Manny uses it.

Mom wouldn't let me and Rodrick take any electronics on the trip, even though they barely take up any space.

She's always saying kids these days don't know how to socialize because they've constantly got their noses two inches from a screen.

But I'll tell you this: when I have kids, I'm gonna let them play with whatever kind of gadget they WANT. If you ask me, electronics are the key to family happiness.

Even after Mom went through every single item in the driveway and cut out all the things we didn't need, there was STILL way too much to fit in the van.

I suggested we rent one of those giant recreational vehicles, because we could fit all our stuff in it and have room to spare.

The way I see it, if you want the whole family to get along, everyone needs their own space. And with one of those souped-up RVs we could spend WEEKS on the road without even bumping into one another.

But Mom said RVs are too expensive and they get terrible petrol mileage, so that put an end to that idea.

Rodrick said maybe we could get one of those trailers you tow BEHIND the car, which sounded smart to me.

But it was pretty clear Rodrick was imagining the trailer as a sort of mini-apartment for HIMSELF, so that wasn't gonna fly, either.

Then Dad chimed in with his OWN idea. He said we could solve the whole space issue by just putting the stuff that didn't fit in the van into the BOAT, which we could tow behind us.

I think Mom realized there wasn't really another option, so she caved in. But getting the boat into the driveway was easier said than done.

Not only did we have to take all the junk out of the boat, but it turned out there was a TREE growing through the bottom. It took three hours to get the boat out from under the deck, and let me just say Mom did not exactly go out of her way to help.

After we got the boat into the driveway, Dad patched up the hole in the bottom and the crack in the hull with some duct tape.

I just hope we're not going anywhere near water on this trip, though.

Because, as far as I know, the boat didn't come with any life jackets.

Saturday

Even with the added space we got from the boat, the minivan was still pretty full. I sneaked my pillow on board at the last second, because I decided I was entitled to at least ONE luxury item.

I figured Rodrick would want to sit in the back of the van, because whenever we go anywhere as a family he likes to stretch out and take a nap.

Every once in a while we'll forget Rodrick is even back there.

This Easter, we made it halfway through church before Mom realized Rodrick never made it out of the van.

Back when we had a station wagon, me and Rodrick used to sit in the way back TOGETHER, in a seat that faced the rear window. But we got in big trouble when we played a practical joke on Mom and Dad that ended up getting us pulled over by the police.

When we got in the van today, Rodrick offered me the back seat.

I accepted before he could change his mind, but I should've known his offer was too good to be true.

Before we pulled out of the driveway, Mom said we were taking a "special guest" along for the ride. For a second I was worried we were picking someone ELSE up, because with all our stuff in the van they'd have to sit on the ROOF.

But Mom opened her purse and pulled out a piece of paper with a drawing on it.

The drawing was Flat Stanley, a character from a book I read in second grade.

Flat Stanley is a boy who gets squashed by a bulletin board that falls off his bedroom wall in the middle of the night.

And when they pull the bulletin board off him he's as thin as a piece of paper.

I thought it was pretty cool that Flat Stanley could fold himself up and get mailed to his grandma's, or have his brother fly him like a kite.

But I'll tell you this: if Flat Stanley had a brother like RODRICK, I guarantee he wouldn't survive a whole day.

I really liked the book, but it kind of freaked me out, too. One thing it did was give me a deathly fear of bulletin boards.

In second grade, everyone in my class had to colour in a cutout of Flat Stanley and mail him to a friend or relative who lived far away.

Then that person was supposed to take a picture of Flat Stanley in front of something interesting and mail him back with the photo.

My friend Rowley sent Flat Stanley to a bunch of his relatives and got lots of cool pictures back. Rowley even sent him to his uncle who lives in Asia, and he took a picture of Flat Stanley in front of the Great Wall of China.

Well, the first person Mom sent MY Flat Stanley to was her cousin Stacey, who lives out in Seattle. But she probably wasn't the best choice.

Stacey is one of those people who hoard all sorts of stuff, like newspapers and magazines, so Mom should've known that once her cousin got her hands on Flat Stanley he wasn't coming back.

Today, Mom said she was gonna take photos of our new Flat Stanley in front of all the cool places we visit and then make a scrapbook of our trip. And as soon as we got on the highway she started snapping pictures. But she was probably a little too eager, because her first few pictures weren't exactly keepers.

When Mom wasn't taking pictures, Flat Stanley was taped to the front air-conditioning vent. All I can say is he was having a much better ride than I was. The windows in the back of the van don't open, and the vents were blocked by all our luggage, so I wasn't getting ANY cold air.

What made me even MORE uncomfortable was the fact that Mom was in control of the trip. Mom always tries to make things about education, and I knew she was gonna turn this experience into one long lesson.

She's been doing that ever since I was little. I remember when I got scratched by Gramma's cat and Mom tried to turn it into a "teaching moment".

Sure enough, a half hour into the trip today, Mom started in with the educational stuff.

She had borrowed a bunch of CDs from the library that teach Spanish and said we'd use the long stretches on the road to learn a new language as a family.

Mom's always saying that learning a foreign language is the best thing you can do for your brain. That might be true, but I think she should leave the actual TEACHING to the schools.

Mom decided it would be a good idea to expose me to a foreign language early on, so when I was in first grade she would put the Spanish-speaking channels on TV while we ate breakfast.

Mom would repeat whatever they said on the television, but when SHE said the words they came out a little bit different.

I ended up learning all sorts of phrases that weren't right. For example, the way you're SUPPOSED to say "What's your name" in Spanish is "Cómo te llamas". Well, I know that NOW because I learned it in my middle-school Spanish class.

But when I was little Mom taught me that "What's your name" in Spanish is "Te amo", which ACTUALLY means "I love you". I just wish I had known that before I said it to a million different people.

Today, Mom played the first two Spanish CDs, but she got frustrated that no one seemed to be paying attention. So she switched gears and said we were gonna play a car game she read about in her magazine.

The game was called Alphabet Groceries, and you play it like this: the first player has to name an item you can get at the grocery store that starts with the letter "A". The next person has to come up with an item that starts with "B", and so on.

If a player CAN'T come up with an item that starts with their letter, they're out of the game.

Mom said I should go first, so I said "apple", which I guess was kind of an obvious choice. Rodrick was up next, but he said he couldn't come up with any food that started with "B".

I'm pretty sure he was lying to get out of having to play the game, but with Rodrick you never know.

When Rodrick got knocked out, the turn went to Manny, who came up with his word right away.

Mom started clapping, but I pointed out that "bapple" isn't a real word. She said Manny is just learning the alphabet and that we all need to "encourage" him.

I quit in protest, and from then on it was only Manny, Mom and Dad playing. I really wished my earplugs weren't buried in my duffel bag under a pile of suitcases, because the next hour and a half was pretty painful.

All that talk of food was actually getting me kind of hungry, and when I saw a sign for a drive-through place at the next exit I asked Mom if we could pull over. But Mom said we wouldn't be stopping at any of THOSE kinds of restaurants, because they don't serve "real food".

She said fast-food places lure kids in with cheap plastic toys to trick them into eating sugar and fat, and we weren't gonna fall into that trap. Mom said she had a MUCH better alternative and handed me a lunch bag with my name on it.

Mom said she got the Mommy Meal idea from "Family Frolic", which I guess should not have come as a surprise.

Inside the bag was a tuna sandwich, an orange and a little carton of milk, plus something wrapped in tinfoil.

Mom said I had to eat my fruit before I unwrapped the tinfoil, because that was my "prize".

But I wish I had just opened it right away, because I wouldn't have eaten the whole orange if I'd known the prize was a pack of maths flash cards.

Rodrick got flash cards in HIS lunch, too, and we could both see where this was headed. So, before Mom could turn the next hour of the trip into a tutoring session, I pulled out one of the games Mom had packed in a big tote bag.

The game I grabbed was called "I Must Confess", and when Mom saw it she got so excited she forgot all about the flash cards.

I read the rules, which were pretty simple: one person takes a card from the deck and reads it out loud to everyone else.

If one of the players has done the thing that's written on the card, they earn a point. And the first player to get ten points wins.

I was a little sceptical at first, but I have to admit the game was actually kind of FUN. I learned a lot of things about Mom and Dad I never knew before.

I found out that Dad had a pet chameleon when he was a kid and that Mom dyed her hair blonde once, which really surprised me.

Believe it or not, even RODRICK was getting into the game. He got a point for being the only person who'd ever slept out overnight for tickets to a concert, and ANOTHER point for getting a bug stuck in his ear, which I remember like it was yesterday.

Dad and Rodrick were neck and neck with nine points, and whoever scored next would win the game. Mom seemed really happy everyone was getting along and having fun.

Then she pulled a new card out of the deck and read it.

I'm pretty sure Mom thought no one was gonna get a point on that card, because she was already reaching for the next one. But Rodrick started acting like he had just won the lottery.

Mom thought Rodrick was lying to get a point, but he told her it was TRUE. He said that a few months ago he and his bandmates toilet-papered Mrs Tuttle's house next door after she called the police to complain they were making too much noise rehearsing.

Rodrick thought the whole thing was pretty funny, but Mom didn't seem amused.

LET ME GET THIS STRAIGHT: YOU AND TWO OF YOUR BANDMATES TOILET-PAPERED AN ELDERLY WOMAN'S HOUSE?

If I was Rodrick, I would've changed my story real quick and said I was just joking around to win the game. But Rodrick didn't seize his chance to bail out.

Mom had Dad pull over to the side of the road, then handed Rodrick her phone and made him call Mrs Tuttle to apologize, which was awkward for everyone in the car.

After that, it was quiet in the van for a long time. Mom was about to pop the next Spanish CD in the stereo, but luckily Manny had fallen asleep by then, so she couldn't.

If you wake Manny up in the middle of one of his naps, he'll go completely ballistic, and there's NO calming him down. So whenever Manny falls asleep Mom and Dad do everything they can to KEEP him that way.

I was big on naps when I was Manny's age, too. I used to take an hour-long nap after lunch every day, and when I started pre-school we had an official nap time where everyone pulled out a mat and slept on the floor.

If you ask me, I think they should give kids nap time all the way through college. But they stop doing it after pre-school, which I found out the HARD way.

On the first day of kindergarten, after we had our snacks, I asked the teacher where the mats were, so we could lie down and recharge our batteries.

But she said kindergartners don't HAVE nap time, and I thought she was just making a funny joke.

A few minutes later, the whole class was making paper-bag puppets. Apparently, I was the only one who didn't get the heads-up about the no-nap thing, because for the rest of the day everyone else seemed fine, while I could barely function.

I'm glad Mom remembered to bring a dummy on the trip, because as long as Manny's got one stuck in his mouth he can sleep through just about anything. Manny lost his favourite dummy last night, but Dad ran out to get a new one at a store near our house that sells gag gifts.

I guess it looks a little strange, but it works just as well as a regular one.

Manny had been sleeping peacefully for about an hour today when we stopped at a tollbooth. Dad rolled down his window to get a ticket, and the guy in the booth had such a loud voice he sounded like he was speaking through a MEGAPHONE.

Manny started to fuss, and his dummy came halfway out of his mouth. But luckily Rodrick reacted quickly, and Manny fell back asleep.

I think Mom was a little frustrated that Manny was napping in the first place. She had marked a bunch of places on her map where she wanted us to stop and get out for some sightseeing, but now we had to keep driving.

The problem I had with Manny's nap was that I really needed to get out of the car and stretch, but I COULDN'T.

I tried to make myself comfortable, but, with all the stuff piled around me, it was impossible.

Luckily, my backpack was in arm's reach behind my seat, because it had some books and other things I'd brought to entertain myself.

Mom's always trying to get me to read stuff that's "enriching", but when it comes to books I know what I like. And, ever since elementary school, my favourite books have been the ones in the Underpants Bandits series.

The Underpants Bandits books are about these two kids named Bryce and Brody who go back in time and steal underwear from famous people so they can put the underpants in a museum.

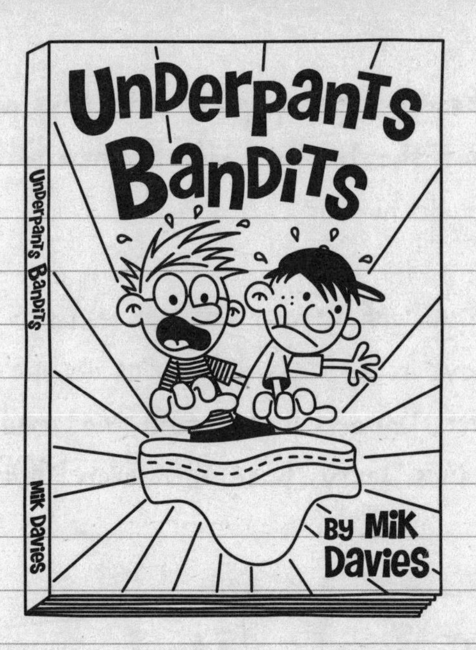

I know that sounds kind of ridiculous, but the books are actually pretty funny.

The books are super popular with boys at my school, but the teachers HATE them because of all the "rude humour".

Whenever a book report was due in fifth grade, all the boys in my class did theirs on one of the Underpants Bandits books. And that made my teacher, Mrs Terry, hate them even MORE.

Our class had a project where we had to write a letter to our favourite author, and of course all the boys chose Mik Davies.

But Mrs Terry said we had to pick someone ELSE, so I grabbed a random book from the library and wrote my letter to an author I'd never even heard of before.

March 30th

Dear Nathaniel,

My teacher made us write to an author, so I picked you. I have not read any of your books (no offence).

Here are my questions for you:

1. What's your favourite colour?

2. What's your favourite animal?

3. What's your favourite flavour of ice cream?

4. What's your favourite super-hero movie?

I would appreciate it if you could answer me soon, because I am getting graded on this.

Sincerely,

Greg Heffley

But I probably should've checked the year the book was written before I wrote my letter.

May 20th

Dear Mr Heffley,

We regret to inform you that the author to whom you have written, Mr Hawthorne, passed away more than a century ago.

As such, he will not be able to respond to your questions.

With regrets,

Katrina Welker
Publisher

Most PARENTS don't like the Underpants Bandits books, either.

In fact, the PTA had a meeting that year where they decided parents' tax dollars shouldn't be used to purchase any of the Underpants Bandits books for the library.

When we came back to school from spring break, all of the Underpants Bandits books in the library were GONE.

I hope these adults are happy when a whole generation of boys grow up not knowing how to read.

When the school banned the Underpants Bandits books, it just made them more popular than EVER. Some boys sneaked in copies from home and passed them on to OTHER kids.

One kid even brought in a bootleg copy of an Underpants Bandits book from Japan. I couldn't understand a word of it, but it was pretty easy to figure out from the pictures what was going on.

I actually wrote to the author on my OWN just to tell him how much I liked his series.

August 18th

Dear Mr Davies,

I'm just writing to tell you, don't listen to these people who say your books are garbage, because they don't know what they're talking about. I know a bunch of kids (including me) who think your books are great.

As far as the "rude humour" goes, I find that stuff hilarious, so please don't change a thing. In fact, I would encourage you to put MORE bodily functions and things of that nature in your books.

Sincerely,

Greg Heffley

I'd never written a fan letter like that, and every day when I got home from school I ran to the mailbox to see if Mik Davies had written me back.

I finally got a response almost a year later, and I was really excited.

But when I read the letter it was a HUGE disappointment.

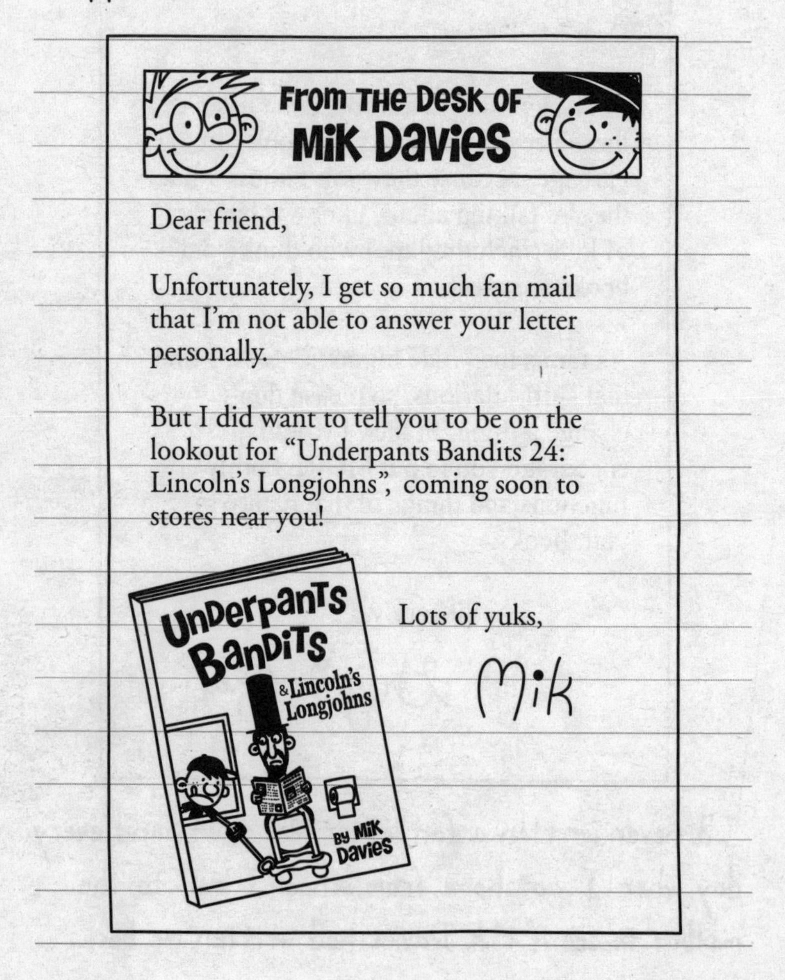

FROM THE DESK OF MIK DAVIES

Dear friend,

Unfortunately, I get so much fan mail that I'm not able to answer your letter personally.

But I did want to tell you to be on the lookout for "Underpants Bandits 24: Lincoln's Longjohns", coming soon to stores near you!

Lots of yuks,

Mik

I couldn't believe I poured my heart out to this guy and all I got back was an AD.

Even though that whole experience left a bad taste in my mouth, I still like his books.

At least I get to read whatever I WANT this summer. Rodrick's school gave him a whole list of required reading, and some of the books look like a lot of work.

But Rodrick's not much of a reader, so he rented all the MOVIE versions of the books on his list.

Mom said it's not smart to watch the movie without reading the book, because they usually change a lot of stuff. But Rodrick said as long as he got the basic idea, he'd be fine.

I think his approach is gonna cause problems, though. "The Lord of the Rings" is on his summer reading list, but when he rented the movie he wasn't careful about checking the title.

Rodrick watched the movie TWICE, and after the second time he told Mom that whoever wrote the book must be a genius. But I'm guessing Rodrick's teacher is gonna be pretty confused when she reads his book report in September.

By the time I was done reading today, I really needed to get out of the car to prevent my legs from permanently cramping.

Manny was still asleep, but he had somehow turned himself all the way upside down in his seat.

When Mom noticed, she told Dad maybe we should stop driving for the day, so he pulled off at the next exit.

I was really looking forward to eating a meal at a decent restaurant, but Mom said we're on a budget and tonight we were gonna pick up our dinner at a grocery store.

Dad found a supermarket a few miles from the exit. But Mom was afraid that if the van stopped moving Manny would wake up and have a fit. So Mom wrote out a shopping list for Rodrick and gave him some money, then Dad drove real slow in front of the entrance so Rodrick could hop out.

Dad had to circle the parking lot about ten times, which wasn't easy since we were towing a boat. Eventually, Rodrick came out with a couple of bags of groceries. And, from the looks of it, he picked up some extra items for himself.

When Dad pulled the van round, Rodrick hopped in. Then we started looking for a place to stay for the night, but the selection in the area wasn't that great.

A few of the motels had big signs that said they had "Colour TV", which if you ask me is not anything to brag about in this day and age.

Dad finally pulled over at a place with air-conditioning and a pool, which sounded pretty good to me, especially considering that I'd lost about five pounds in sweat sitting in the back seat.

I haven't stayed in a whole lot of motels, but, if I had to guess, I'd say we picked one on the lower end of the spectrum.

The lobby smelled like mildew, and the carpet was covered in weird stains.

But everyone was too tired to get back in the car and look for another place to stay.

We got the key to our room, and when we walked in it reeked of smoke. There were little holes in the covers and pillows that I'm pretty sure were cigarette burns.

Dad picked a towel up off the floor, then dropped it because it was WET.

Mom went back to the front desk and asked for a different room, but the clerk said the motel was full and that we'd got the last one.

Mom told her in that case we were gonna leave and take our business to another motel. But the clerk told her there was a twenty-four-hour cancellation policy, so we couldn't get our money back.

When Mom returned to the room, she said we were gonna have to try to make the best of a bad situation. Then she and Dad stripped the bed down to the bare mattress.

Believe it or not, Manny slept through ALL of this. Mom said that if he woke up now he'd be awake all night, so she was just gonna let him sleep through till morning.

Mom put Manny down in the middle of the sofa bed and pulled a blanket over him.

The rest of us were really hungry, so we emptied out the groceries Rodrick bought. But it turned out he didn't buy ANYTHING on Mom's list.

Rodrick was supposed to get sandwich supplies, orange juice and stuff like that, but he just got a bunch of things HE likes.

Mom was pretty upset that Rodrick didn't get a single thing on the list she gave him, but his excuse was that he couldn't read her handwriting. Mom told him it wasn't very smart to get cinnamon rolls and a frozen pizza, since those things needed an oven and we didn't HAVE one.

But Rodrick said we could MICROWAVE the pizza. Then he put it inside the microwave oven to prove it.

At least, Rodrick THOUGHT it was a microwave. It was actually a SAFE. By the time he figured that out, the pizza was locked inside.

Mom gave me what was left of her cash and said to go down to the vending machine to get the most nutritious stuff I could find.

And that's how we ended up eating sugar wafers and breath mints for dinner on the first night of our road trip.

Sunday

Last night we couldn't watch TV or do anything in the room because Manny was asleep on the pullout sofa.

Mom wouldn't even let us keep the light on, so we all sat in the dark for a while until me and Rodrick decided to go down to the pool to kill some time.

Well, the sign outside the motel said there was a pool, but there was no actual WATER in it.

And it didn't look like there HAD been for at least five years.

There was a hot tub near the pool that DID have water in it, but some family was already using it. So me and Rodrick waited our turn.

Unfortunately, the family couldn't take a hint that we wanted to use the hot tub, so eventually me and Rodrick just went back to the room.

The lights were still out, and Mom and Dad were asleep on the mattress. I guess they must've been pretty exhausted, because they were still wearing all their clothes.

With Mom and Dad on the bed and Manny on the sofa, it didn't leave a lot of good sleep options for me and Rodrick.

We checked the closet for a cot or an air mattress, but there was nothing.

Rodrick was one step ahead of me, though. He gathered up the sofa cushions and made a bed for himself on the floor. Five seconds later, he was out cold.

I figured the closet was as good a place as any for me to sleep, so I got some towels out of the bathroom and laid them on the floor.

After lying there for a minute, I noticed a TERRIBLE smell and thought a mouse must've died in the vent or something.

I tried covering my nose with a washcloth, but that seemed to make the smell even WORSE.

It was hard enough trying to fall asleep under those conditions, but then someone in the room started SNORING. Luckily, I was prepared for that. Mom and Dad BOTH snore, which is the reason I thought ahead and brought earplugs on the trip.

But it was so dark in the room I could only find ONE in my duffel bag, so I had to try sleeping with the earplug in my left ear and my other ear pressed to the floor.

I did actually fall asleep for a few minutes, but woke up to some kind of ruckus going on outside.

When I looked out of the peephole, I saw something flash by, but I couldn't tell what it was. So I cracked open the door to see what was going on.

It turns out those kids from the hot tub had got their hands on a cleaning cart and were ramming it into a wall.

I couldn't BELIEVE these kids' parents were letting them run wild in the middle of the night, so I stepped out of the room and went over to give them a piece of my mind.

The littlest kid burst into tears and ran into his room, and I didn't feel bad for even one second. But a minute later his door opened again, and his FATHER came out.

I wasn't about to get yelled at by a grown man in his underwear, so I ran back to our room and locked the door. Then I prayed with all my might that the chain lock was strong enough to keep him out.

I guess the kids' dad didn't see which door I went into, because he knocked on the wrong one. Then he pounded on the door right next to ours before giving up and going back to his room.

Once the coast was clear, I hung a little sign on our doorknob in case the guy decided to come BACK.

It was REALLY hard falling asleep after that, because every time I heard someone outside the door I held my breath until they passed by.

Before I knew it, the sun was up and so was Manny. Mom turned on the television, and whenever Manny watches TV he TALKS to it.

I was a little annoyed with Manny blabbering away, but I guess I can't complain. I used to do the same exact thing when I was younger.

One time when I was watching my favourite show, the host asked a question.

I was just goofing around when I answered, but the guy on TV actually RESPONDED.

I wish it never happened, though. Because for a long time after that I thought the people inside the TV could hear everything I said.

In fact, on my sixth birthday, Mom had to sit me down and have a talk about the difference between "imaginary" friends and "real" friends.

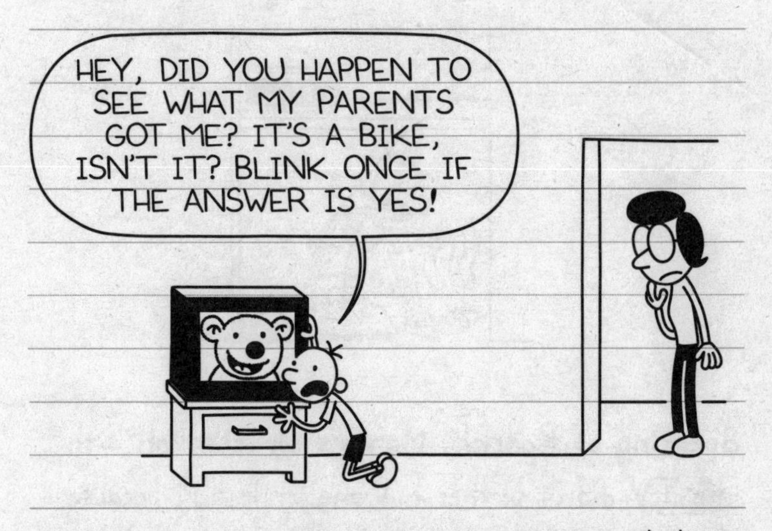

Once Manny got going in a conversation with his favourite TV characters this morning, I knew there was no point in trying to fall back asleep. So I just got up for the day.

And, when I did, I found out the source of that awful smell. Rodrick had put his shoes in the closet, and I had spent the whole night breathing in his fumes.

But even WORSE was that the "washcloth" I had used to block the smell was actually one of Rodrick's SOCKS.

Speaking of Rodrick, Manny's conversation with the TV didn't bother him one little bit, because he just slept right through all the noise.

Dad was getting a little restless waiting for everyone to get going this morning. He's one of those guys who gets up every day at the crack of dawn so he can arrive at his office early, and this whole late-start thing wasn't working for him.

Eventually, Mom made Rodrick get up and take a shower. We went to a diner right next to the motel for breakfast, then got back in the van.

Mom said that from now on we were all gonna be on the same sleep schedule so we wouldn't waste any more time on our trip. But, before she was even done talking, Manny passed out in his car seat.

Mom's big plan for the day was for us to go to a country fair she read about in "Family Frolic".

I'd never been to anything like that before, but it looked like it was worth checking out.

The fair was a few hours away, so that meant me being cramped in the back seat again, which was starting to get old. Thankfully, after an hour, Mom offered to switch places with me.

When I got up to the front seat, I couldn't believe how much ROOM there was.

And it wasn't just all the space that was awesome. I even had individual temperature settings and my own cup holder.

I went to change the radio station, but Dad stopped me. He said only the DRIVER gets to pick the music. I didn't think that was fair, but I wasn't gonna complain and risk getting sent to the back seat.

Dad's music was pretty awful, but the view totally made up for it.

When you're in the back, you don't have any sense of what's ahead. Sitting up front, I had a whole new perspective and could almost see why Mom was so gung ho about taking this road trip.

When we took the exit for the country fair, we came to a stoplight. We were behind a minivan that was the same exact model as ours, only purple.

The kids in the van looked kind of familiar. It took me a second to realize they were the same ones from last night.

I hadn't told Mom and Dad about the incident with the kids and the cleaning cart, because I was worried I wouldn't come out looking too great. And they definitely didn't need to know about my run-in with Mr Beardo.

The kids in the purple van recognized me right away and started making obnoxious faces.

I wasn't gonna just sit there and take it from those little punks, so I made a face at THEM.

The skinny one made the same face back at ME, and the second he did the light turned green and they accelerated. When their van lurched forward, the little kid face-planted into the back window.

Dad passed them on the left, and Mr Beardo got a good look at me.

Luckily, the parking lot for the fair was only a few hundred feet up the road. Once we stopped, I wanted to stay inside until I was sure we weren't being tailed by the purple van.

But it looked like we were in the clear. Manny was still asleep in his car seat, so Mom said she'd stay back with him and the rest of us could go on ahead.

The fair was a LOT different than I thought it was gonna be. I expected it to have a Ferris wheel and a merry-go-round and stuff like that, but instead there were a bunch of tents with farm animals and booths with homemade food.

We were getting kind of hungry anyway, so we went looking for something to eat.

They had corn dogs and doughnuts and all the stuff you'd expect at a big fair. But then they had crazy things like deep-fried butter on a stick.

I was actually glad Mom was still in the van, because I was pretty sure that kind of thing didn't qualify as "real food" in her book.

After about an hour of walking the fairground, Dad went back to the car to see if Manny was awake yet, and he told me and Rodrick to go explore on our own.

The two of us wandered around for a while until we came across a tent where there was something big going on.

It was a Foulest Footwear contest, and they were offering a prize for whoever had the nastiest shoe.

There was a big line of people ready to submit their entries.

I told Rodrick HE should enter, because if ANYONE deserved to win this thing, it was him.

While we were waiting in line, me and Rodrick got in an argument over who would get to keep the prize. I said we should split it 50-50 because it was my idea, but he said he should get the whole thing because it was HIS shoe and he was the one who made it stink.

Right before we got to the judging table, we reached a compromise where I'd get 10% of the prize as Rodrick's agent.

Some of the other shoes looked a lot worse than Rodrick's, and I was losing confidence that he'd win. But when the judges got to the smell test it was all over.

Rodrick won first prize, which turned out to be a coupon for one deep-fried butter on a stick. I told Rodrick he could have it all to himself, because the thought of eating any more butter made me feel a little nauseous.

Rodrick asked the judges for his shoe back, but they said they were gonna send it on to the national competition. So that left Rodrick walking around with only one shoe. I decided to explore the nearby stalls while Rodrick was polishing off his stick of fried butter.

But I had a SERIOUSLY close call when I turned a corner and almost ran smack into the entire Beardo family. Luckily, I was able to duck for cover just in time.

Now that I knew the Beardos were at the fairground, I was eager to get out of there.

I went to look for Rodrick, but he must've gone back to the van. I decided to head there myself, but on my way out I spotted the top of Mom's head in a crowd under one of the livestock tents.

People were packed shoulder to shoulder, and I tried pushing my way through to get to where Mom was.

But, when I got halfway in, a big cheer went up.

When I finally made it up to the front, I was surprised to see Manny standing in the middle of the crowd, holding a piece of paper.

Apparently, there was a contest to see who could come the closest to guessing the weight of a hog, and Manny got it exactly right.

The prize for guessing the hog's weight was a real live baby pig.

Mom explained to the judge that they'd just entered the contest for fun and didn't actually WANT the pig.

But the people in the crowd seemed kind of insulted and wouldn't take no for an answer.

With all the commotion this was causing, I was nervous the Beardo family was gonna come over to the livestock tent to see what was going on. Luckily, by then Mom seemed ready to get out of there herself, and we made our way to the exit.

Dad was sitting in the van with the air-conditioning cranked up, and when he saw Mom carrying a pig he was a little taken by surprise.

Mom filled Dad in on how Manny won the pig in the contest, but he didn't seem too thrilled with the news.

Dad said we had no business owning a pig and that we needed to take it back to the fair immediately.

But Mom said it was too late, because the pig had already "imprinted" on Manny.

Dad still wasn't on board, though. He said a pig is a "barn animal" and could be carrying all sorts of parasites and whatnot. But Mom said a LOT of people keep pigs as pets, and she'd heard they're just as smart as dogs.

Then Rodrick got in on the conversation. He voted for KEEPING the pig because he said we could get free bacon from it every morning, the way you get eggs from a chicken.

So either he doesn't understand how pigs work, or he just wasn't thinking it all the way through.

I was all in favour of keeping the pig if it meant we could hurry up and get going.

I noticed a purple van parked a few spaces away from ours, and I was nervous the Beardos would show up any second.

Dad finally caved in. He said if we were gonna keep the pig it would have to ride in the boat. But Mom said putting the pig in the boat was "inhumane" and that we needed to find a place for it in the van.

The thing is there wasn't anywhere to PUT the pig in the van. We couldn't just let it roam free, and we couldn't exactly strap it in with a seat belt, either. So Mom emptied out the cooler and put the pig in THERE.

Once that was settled, we finally pulled out of the parking lot.

After we put a few miles between us and the fair, I could finally breathe again.

But the pig started causing trouble right away. By the time we got back on the highway it had tipped over the cooler and was rooting around in one of the Mommy Meal bags.

I had to wrangle the pig back into the cooler, and THIS time I strapped the seat belt across it so it wouldn't tip over.

Mom figured the pig was hungry, so she said we needed to stop and get it some food. Her idea was for us to go to a restaurant and then give the pig our leftovers. That sounded like a good deal to me, since it meant we'd actually get to have a sit-down dinner.

We found a place to eat a few miles away, and Mom stayed back in the van with the pig while the rest of us went inside. But when the waitress saw that Rodrick was only wearing one shoe she said she couldn't serve him.

Dad said me and Rodrick could take turns using MY shoe. But I wish I hadn't let Rodrick go first, because he's the world's slowest eater.

When we got back in the van, we gave the pig our leftover corn and vegetables, which it ate straight out of the styrofoam container.

Mom started looking up places to stay for the night on the GPS. She asked Rodrick to call a hotel to see if they had any rooms available. They did, but Rodrick blew it by getting too specific.

Mom found another place a few miles away, and this time she did the talking.

The hotel was just after the tolls. A few hundred feet from the exit, traffic came to a crawl.

That was a problem for me because I had two big glasses of lemonade at the restaurant and REALLY needed to use the bathroom.

I spotted a petrol station up ahead and asked Mom and Dad if I could hop out and use the bathroom, then catch up with the car after I was done.

Dad didn't like the idea because he was worried that by the time I got back they might already be through the tollbooth. By now it was pretty obvious the pig needed to go, too, because it was running in little circles inside the cooler.

Mom said I could use the bathroom at the petrol station as long as I brought the pig WITH me.

So I tucked it under my arm and ran across three lanes of traffic to the petrol station.

I tried the handle to the men's room, but it was locked. I waited for the person using it to come OUT, but whoever was in there wasn't in any rush to wrap things up.

I was getting kind of desperate, so I tried the handle to the women's room, but THAT was locked, too.

I ran back to the car, which had only moved forward about five feet in the time I was gone.

When I told Mom that both bathrooms were occupied, she said petrol-station bathrooms are ALWAYS locked and that I had to ask the ATTENDANT for the key.

So I ran BACK to the petrol station and told the guy at the desk I needed to use the restroom in a hurry.

I'm not sure what I was expecting from a petrol-station bathroom, but it was actually a lot WORSE than I could've even imagined.

Let me just say it was pretty awkward using the toilet with a farm animal staring right at me. But the pig was even MORE embarrassed than I was, because when it was the pig's turn to go nothing happened.

After I gave the key back to the attendant, I spotted our van just as it was about to go through the tollbooth. So I sprinted all the way across traffic to get to it in time.

But, before I opened the door, I wish I had noticed that the van didn't have a BOAT attached to it.

OUR van was actually still a few cars back and, by the time I got inside, the pig looked like he was about to burst.

I guess Mom was right about pigs being smart, because when I put him on Manny's potty seat he knew EXACTLY what to do.

Monday

When we pulled up to the hotel last night, I was relieved that it looked a lot nicer than the place we stayed the night BEFORE.

Mom and Dad weren't taking any chances on getting turned away at the desk because of the pig, so we kept it in the cooler until we got into our room.

I think Mom felt bad about the sleep situation at the motel the first night, because this time she rented TWO rooms so everyone would have a bed.

But I should've known there was a catch. Mom said, since she and Dad had Manny in THEIR room, the pig was gonna have to stay in OURS.

I didn't know what I was supposed to do with the pig, so I tried putting it in our bathtub. But it started whimpering the second I set it down.

I decided to let the pig loose in the bathroom, but when I peeked inside a few minutes later it had made a TERRIBLE mess in there. And I'm pretty sure it ate a bar of soap, too.

I let the pig free in the bedroom so I could keep an eye on it, but the first thing it did was go straight to the door connecting the two rooms.

Eventually, Dad got sick of all the noise and opened the door to let the pig in.

I was so tired I fell asleep before my head hit the pillow.

This morning I woke up to the sound of weird noises coming from the foot of my bed. At first I thought Rodrick had got up early, but then I realized the sound was coming from the PIG.

It had somehow figured out how to open the minibar door and was rooting through the candy and other snacks inside.

I picked the pig up and put it in our bathtub, then went next door to tell Mom and Dad what happened. But it turned out the pig had raided THEIR minibar, too.

Somehow it had even got into the DRINKS. I counted at least three empty cans on the floor, and don't even ask me how a pig managed to do THAT.

Dad went down to the front desk to tell them our "pet" had got into the minibar and we shouldn't be charged for all the stuff it ate.

But the clerk told Dad we were gonna have to pay for the stuff from the minibar and, on top of THAT, there was a fifty-dollar penalty for violating the hotel's "no pet" policy.

After the final tally, the pig ended up costing us more than the ROOMS did.

Mom was eager to get on the road, so she woke Rodrick up and told him to get in the shower. But I probably should've mentioned to him that the pig was in the bathtub before he stepped in.

When we got in the car, Dad was on the phone with his office. Apparently, there was some sort of emergency, and he was the only one who knew how to take care of it.

Mom had planned a big day for us with lots of stops, so she wasn't happy that Dad had to deal with a work situation. But we hit the road anyway, and Dad talked on the phone while he drove.

Our first stop was a place that claimed to have the largest piece of popcorn in the world, which ended up not being that impressive. First of all, it wasn't a real piece of popcorn – it was a wood carving. And, second, it wasn't even all that big.

When we got out of the car, Dad stayed back on his call. The pig stayed, too, sleeping off the drinks from the minibar.

Next we went to a place that's supposedly "world famous" because it has life-size carvings of all the US presidents in butter.

This time Mom made Dad get out of the van and join us, but he stayed on the phone the whole time.

When we got back in the car, Mom let Dad know it wasn't OK for him to be missing out on "family time". Dad told her he just needed to deal with one more work issue and, after it was taken care of, he'd give us his full attention.

Dad said he was about to get a call from one of his international clients and that when he DID it was really important for everyone to stay quiet so it would seem like Dad was in the office.

It didn't look like that was gonna be a big problem. Manny was already down for his afternoon nap, and the pig was still passed out in the cooler.

A few minutes later, Dad's call came in. You could tell by how loud the guy was talking that he was upset. But Dad spoke in an even tone, and his client seemed to calm down.

The rest of us stayed as quiet as we could. But then Rodrick got out one of his packs of bubble gum and put all five pieces in his mouth and started chewing it real loud.

Mom snapped her fingers to try to get him to stop making so much noise.

But her finger snapping was actually LOUDER than the gum chewing, which you could tell was irritating Dad.

Mom wanted Rodrick to get rid of his gum, so she pressed the button to open the sunroof. But when she DID the sound of air blowing inside the van was like a jet turbine.

Mom realized she had made a mistake, so she pressed the button to CLOSE the sunroof. But, before it shut all the way, Rodrick chucked his gum through the opening.

The gum boomeranged right BACK and got stuck in the gear track of the sunroof.

Mom frantically pressed the "close" button, but the sunroof was jammed open. At that moment, the air rushing in from outside dislodged Flat Stanley from the vent, and he went flying.

Dad was having a really hard time concentrating on his call and was fumbling with the buttons to try to shut the sunroof himself.

But now he didn't have a hand on the wheel and was steering with his KNEES.

Dad started drifting out of his lane, and the driver of a huge tractor-trailer let us know it, which made Dad drop his phone.

The horn also startled Manny, and his dummy popped out and on to the floor.

Manny was sucking air like he still had his dummy in his mouth, and I knew we had about ten seconds to find it before he had a full-on tantrum.

I spotted the dummy on the floor in front of me and tried to unfasten my seat belt so I could reach it. But instead I accidentally unbuckled the seat belt holding the COOLER in place.

Dad was trying to reach for his phone at the same time, and he jerked the car to the left, which made the cooler tip over.

Now it was total chaos. The pig was loose, Manny was crying and Dad was cursing because he couldn't reach his phone.

But the main problem was the PIG. It was going bananas, running around on the floor and squealing like crazy. Everyone was trying to grab it, but the pig was too slippery.

Then, all of a sudden, the pig went quiet. And when he popped back up we knew why.

I reached out real slow and plucked Manny's dummy out of the pig's mouth. And that's when it BIT me.

I guess the pig decided this was its chance to make a run for it. It hopped up on Manny's seat and tried to squeeze through the window, which was open a crack.

The pig managed to get its head and front legs out of the window and would've made it ALL the way out if Mom hadn't jumped over her seat and grabbed its hind legs.

But when she lunged for the pig she kicked a button on the stereo, and now we had the Spanish CD blaring at full volume.

The whole time, Dad was swerving all over the place. Eventually, Mom got the pig back inside and closed Manny's window. Dad managed to pull the van over and turn off the stereo.

It was quiet in the car for a full minute while everyone caught their breath. Dad was really mad that we messed up his business call, and he let us know it.

But he probably should've made sure his phone was off first. Because when he put it to his ear his client was still on the other end.

Tuesday

After Dad's work-call disaster yesterday, he and Mom had a long talk outside the car. Then they got back in, and we drove in silence for a while.

Half an hour later, we pulled into the parking lot of a petting zoo. Mom opened the side door and took the cooler with the pig in it out of the van.

Mom went inside, and five minutes later she came out with an empty cooler.

Personally, I wasn't sad to see the pig go, but Manny was a different story.

I'm not so sure Mom was doing the petting zoo any favours by donating a pig that bites kids.

And, speaking of which, my finger was really KILLING me.

Dad said that the pig probably hadn't had any immunizations and might even have rabies, which was NOT what I wanted to hear.

I've seen enough horror movies to know that when a person gets bitten by an animal nothing good comes of it. The LAST thing I need is to turn into some kind of were-pig, because that could really mess up my dating life.

Mom took a look at my finger, and I could tell she was a little worried. She said we should find a doctor to check it out, which didn't calm my nerves any.

Mom tried to find an emergency-care place on the GPS, but there was nothing within a fifty-mile radius.

But she DID find a VETERINARIAN'S office five minutes up the road.

She said a veterinarian would have the same stuff as a regular doctor, but a vet could actually be BETTER because they might know a thing or two about pig bites.

I honestly thought Mom was joking around about this veterinarian thing, but she was dead serious. And a few minutes later we pulled into the parking lot.

Mom talked to the receptionist at the front desk while the rest of us waited on a bench.

A minute later, Mom came back with a clipboard and some paperwork to fill out.

All I can say is I hope this stuff doesn't get filed on my permanent record, because if it crops up later in life it could be embarrassing.

Emergency Pet Care

Patient Registration

Pet's name: "Greg"

Owner's name: Susan Heffley

Species: Human

Last vaccination: January 12

History of worms? Yes ☒ No ☐
as a toddler

Last rabies shot: N/A

Spayed/Neutered? Yes ☐ No ☒

Once Mom handed in the forms, the receptionist told me I could sit with the other "patients" to wait for the doctor.

You'd think I'd get some sort of priority because I'm a human being, but I got put behind a gerbil that had swallowed a cigarette and a cat that had got its face stuck in a yogurt container.

When we had our dog, Sweetie, Mom had to take him to the vet a bunch of times for getting into stuff he wasn't supposed to eat. But the LAST time she took him she didn't really need to.

Mom had found some empty cellophane wrappers from a pack of whoopie pies in the laundry room, and she figured Sweetie had eaten them.

Apparently, chocolate is like POISON to a dog, so Mom rushed him to the vet to get his stomach pumped.

When Mom brought Sweetie home from the vet, she told me he had got into the whoopie pies. I felt kind of bad, because I was the one who ate them, not the dog.

And, from what I've heard, getting your stomach pumped isn't a real pleasant experience.

I feel like my visit to the vet was payback for the whoopie-pie incident, especially when the nurse weighed me on the same scale they use for DOGS.

The nurse took my temperature, too, and had me hold the thermometer under my tongue for thirty seconds.

When I got back to the waiting area, Rodrick told me that when they take an ANIMAL'S temperature they stick the thermometer somewhere ELSE, and they probably use the same one for all their patients.

I was worried Rodrick might be right, but then I realized this information was coming from a guy who was eating gerbil pellets.

Twice while we were waiting at the vet's, Manny bolted out of the front door, and both times Dad grabbed him before he got too far. I think Manny was pretty mad about us leaving his pig at the petting zoo, and he was acting out.

When I was Manny's age, I used to get mad at Mom and Dad and try to run away all the time.

I remember once when we were in the changing room at the pool and Mom was trying to make me wear a bathing suit I didn't like. I took off running, but I wasn't really thinking about where I was GOING.

RODRICK used to run away a lot, too. When he was in first grade, he'd take off every day at the same time, but he'd come back home when Mom told him his favourite TV show was on.

When Manny tried to run away a THIRD time today, Mom bought a retractable leash at the front desk to try to keep him under control.

Mom also got a bandage for Rodrick's foot so we could start going into restaurants as a family again.

Finally, the veterinarian was ready to see me, and the nurse led us into the exam room. My palms started getting sweaty, because I always get a little nervous when it's time to see the doctor.

I'm not a big fan of needles, and Mom knows it. So whenever I need to get a flu shot or something Mom doesn't tell me it's coming.

And by the time I figure out what's going on it's too late.

But there weren't any shots this time round. Mom told the vet what had happened, and she took a look at my finger.

The vet said there was nothing to worry about since the pig's teeth hadn't broken the skin.

She put some antibacterial ointment on my finger just to be safe and then sent me on my way.

I gotta say, I was pretty impressed by the whole veterinarian experience. The doctor was no-nonsense and didn't ambush me with any needles.

I figure when we get back home I might research some veterinarians in our area. I'm not saying I'm definitely going to make the switch, but I do want to see what my options are.

After the vet's, Dad spent some time trying to get the gum out of the sunroof with a popsicle stick. But it was too messy and eventually he gave up.

Dad didn't like not being able to close the sunroof, so he drove around trying to find a mechanic who could fix it. But nobody he talked to would do it for under a hundred bucks.

So Dad went to a grocery store and bought some cellophane and duct tape, and he fashioned his OWN sunroof.

I think Dad was pretty proud of himself for saving money on repairs, especially when it started to rain and his homemade sunroof held up.

But after a while the cellophane started filling with water and bugs.

Eventually, the whole thing gave way, and for once I was glad to be sitting in the back.

We parked under an overpass and waited for the rain to clear up while Manny and Rodrick changed into some dry clothes.

The trip was a total disaster up to this point, and even Mom was ready to admit it.

She said it probably wasn't such a good idea to do everything according to the magazine, and that if we switched things a little maybe we could turn the trip around.

Mom said that from then on we'd go wherever the road took us and we'd make decisions as a FAMILY along the way. She said the rest of the trip could be like those Choose Your Own Adventure books.

I always liked those books, because on every page you get to make a decision that changes the story.

The problem is I never seem to make the choices that get me to a happy ending.

In fact, it seems like no matter WHAT choice I make it's always the WRONG one.

I wasn't so sure about Mom's new approach, but I figured anything was an improvement as long as I didn't get bitten by any more pigs.

After the rainstorm passed, we got back in the car and gave Mom's idea a try. When we reached our first intersection, she asked everyone if we should turn right or left or go straight.

So we held a vote. Me and Rodrick voted to turn right, and that's what we did. And when we got to ANOTHER intersection we voted again, and this time we turned LEFT.

We drove into this little town that had two restaurants, and after we voted we went to one that ended up having the best apple pie I've ever tasted in my life. In fact, it was so good we ordered a SECOND one.

Mom was really pleased with herself for coming up with this new approach and said she was gonna write in to "Family Frolic" and tell THEM about it.

The only person who WASN'T having a good time was MANNY, who still seemed upset about the pig. Mom kept the leash on him even while we were eating, to make sure he didn't try to run away again.

After lunch, Mom asked me to take Manny to the bathroom, which only had one toilet in it. So I waited outside for him to do his business.

Manny was in there for a while, and I started to wonder what was taking him so long.

I finally opened the door, and he was GONE.

Luckily, Dad saw Manny through the front window of the restaurant and scooped him up before it was too late. Because, if it had been another minute or two, who knows HOW far he would've got.

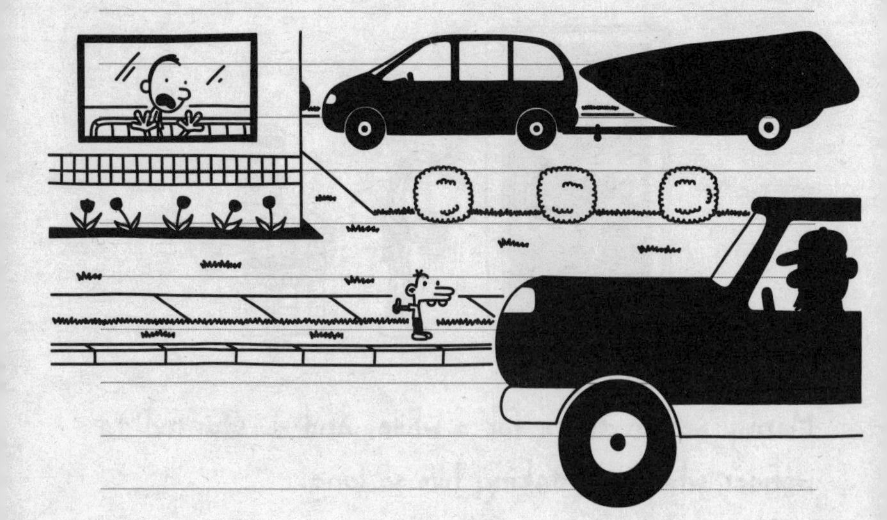

We got back in the van and Mom strapped Manny into his car seat. When we got to a stoplight, everyone agreed that we should go left, and we waited for the light to change.

When it turned green, Dad stepped on the accelerator, but a car came out of nowhere and TOTALLY ran the red light.

Dad laid on the horn, but the driver just kept on going.

Then another car ran the light, and then ANOTHER. It was like nobody even NOTICED that the light was red.

Dad was getting pretty frustrated, and when he saw a gap between two cars he put the pedal to the floor and hung a left.

We barely squeezed in front of the NEXT car, which ALSO ran the light.

When I looked back at the car behind us, I noticed something weird. There was a little flag on either side of the hood.

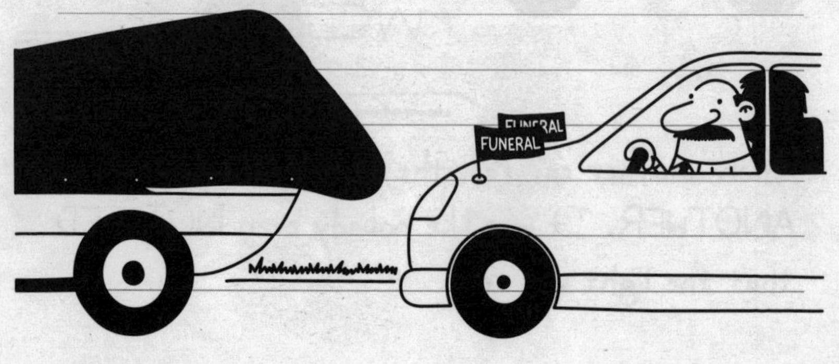

Mom noticed the flags, too, and she got really upset. She said the vehicles behind us were part of a FUNERAL procession.

She explained that during a funeral cars are allowed to go through red lights on their way from the church to the cemetery so they can all stick together. And now we'd gone and cut off the line of cars.

Dad was getting panicky that all the cars behind our van were now following US, and he tried to shake them off our tail by making a few quick turns.

It didn't work, though. Dad said he was gonna get back on the highway and try to lose the cars THAT way, but Mom said the LEAST we could do was lead the people behind us to the cemetery.

So Mom typed "cemetery" into the GPS, and there was one just a few blocks away.

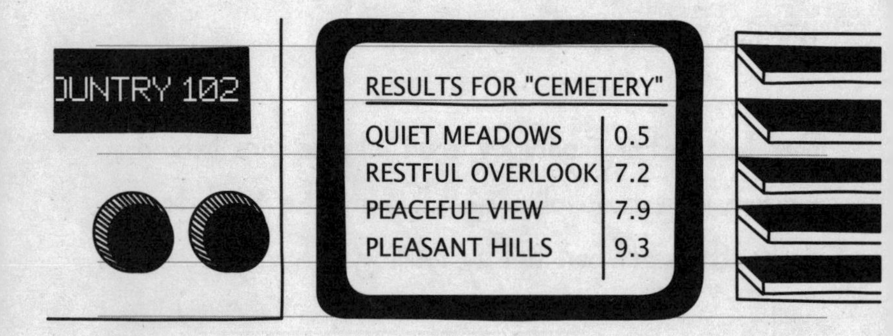

We drove through the gates and parked along the side of the path. Everyone who was following us got out of their cars, but they seemed confused.

One look at the gravestones and it was clear what had happened. Apparently, the GPS treats all cemeteries the same, and it had taken us to a PET cemetery.

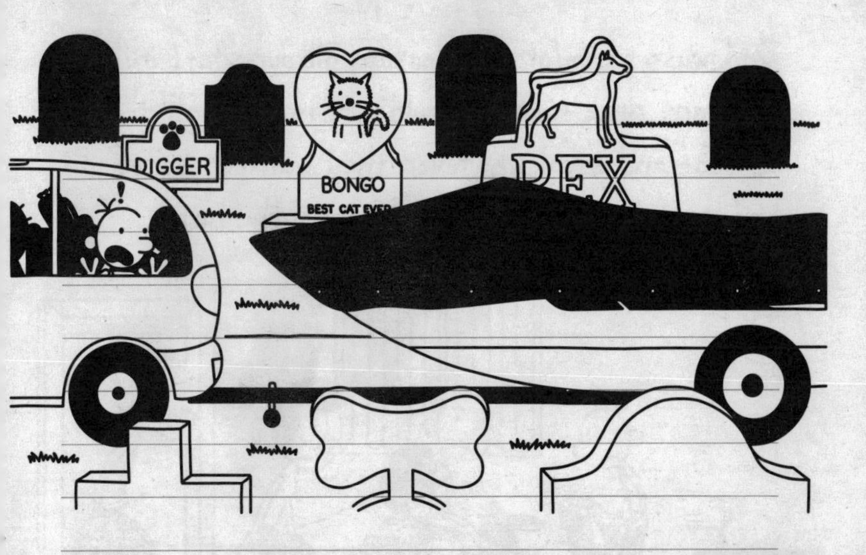

Luckily, Dad got us out of there before things got ugly.

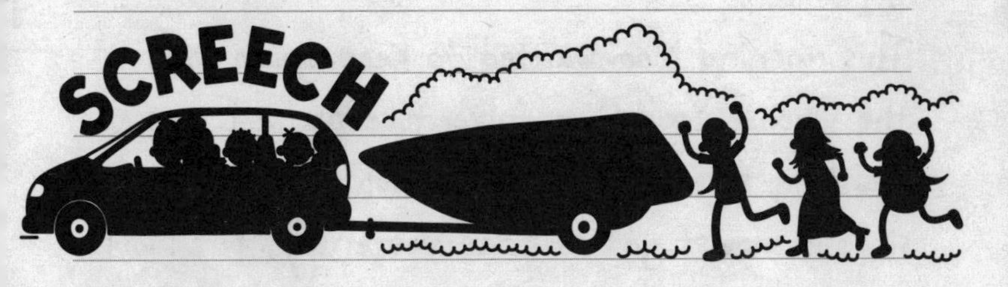

After escaping with our lives from the pet cemetery, everyone decided it would be best to just pack it in for the night. So we found a hotel a few miles away and got a room on the seventh floor.

Dad wasn't comfortable leaving all our stuff in the van, since someone could get in through the sunroof and steal whatever they wanted, so we had to take EVERYTHING into the hotel.

This morning Mom wanted to keep going with the Choose Your Own Adventure plan. I was starting to wonder if it was such a great idea, since it almost got us killed yesterday, but Mom was sticking with it.

She grabbed a bunch of brochures from the front desk and brought them to breakfast so we could figure out what we wanted to do for the day.

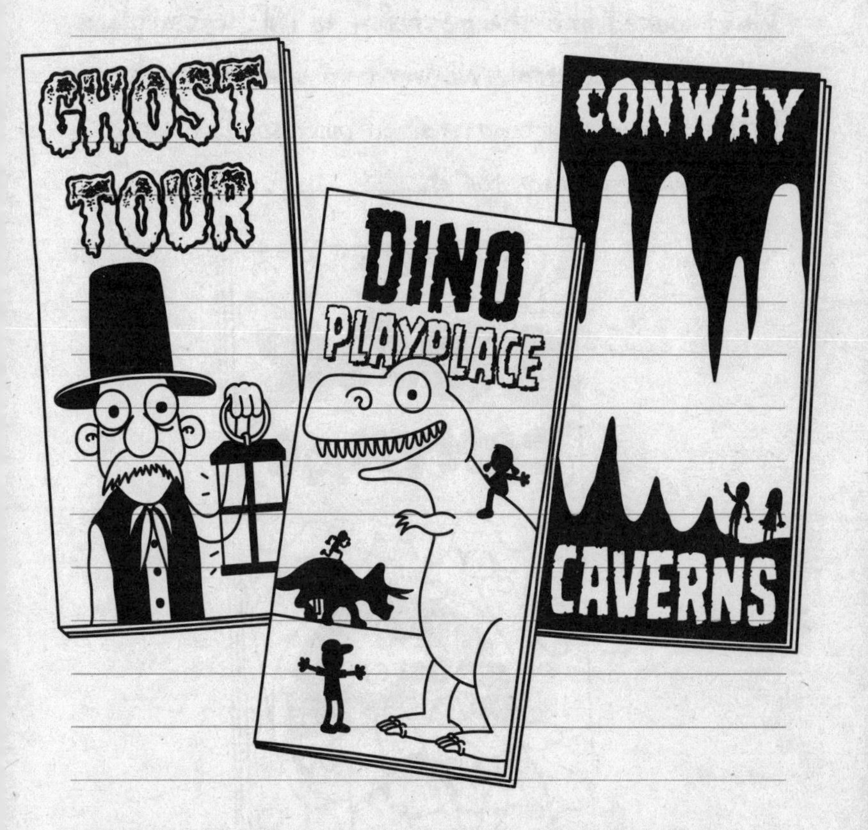

There were actually TOO many options, and nobody could agree on what to do.

Dad wanted to take an all-day guided tour of a Civil War battlefield. Mom wanted to go to the beach. And Rodrick wanted to go to the electric-guitar museum.

What looked like the most fun to ME was a place called Soak Central. We went to a water park LAST summer but got rained out, so I figured this would make up for it.

But Mom read through the brochure and said Soak Central looked "artificial" and that the whole point of this trip was to AVOID places like that.

Since nobody could agree on anything, Mom said she was making an "executive decision" and that we were going to the beach. Dad didn't complain, because I'm sure he was thinking that if we were going to the shore he might actually get a chance to use his BOAT.

I'm really not much of a beach person myself. Whenever we go to one, we bring a blanket and spread it out, then sit there for the whole day. And you can't really go anywhere, because you're worried someone will take your spot.

The last time we went to the beach, Dad brought the tarp he uses to cover the boat so we'd have more room for our family and all our stuff.

But the tarp was at LEAST twice the size of our old blanket, and it took up a ton of space on the beach.

Not to mention the fact that it's made of PLASTIC, so, with the sun beating down, it was like sitting in a frying pan.

It was ESPECIALLY embarrassing when the rest of my family went to grab lunch on the boardwalk and I had to hang back on the tarp by myself to watch our stuff.

So I wasn't real excited about going to the beach, especially since I knew Dad had his boat tarp with him.

The beach was a few hours' drive away, so I decided to take a nap until we got there. And, believe me, with all the junk piled up in the back of the minivan, it wasn't easy.

I woke up when the van slowed down. I thought we were at the beach, but we hadn't even got to the bridge yet. It seemed like everyone had the same idea WE did.

When we were about a quarter of a mile from the bridge, I could tell Dad was starting to get nervous.

He HATES bridges, because for some reason he gets dizzy whenever he has to drive over one.

The bridge to the beach is one of those kinds that's really high above the water, and I'm sure Dad wasn't looking forward to being stuck on it for the next half hour.

Mom told Rodrick HE could drive. So we pulled over and everyone switched seats.

Dad took my place in the back so he wouldn't see the bridge out of the front window, and I moved to the middle row.

When Rodrick got in the driver's seat, he took advantage of Dad's radio rule and blasted heavy-metal music. And I could tell that wasn't helping Dad's nerves.

We were only going about three miles an hour. It looked like we were gonna be stuck on the bridge even longer than I expected, so I opened the bag of cheese curls Rodrick bought at the grocery store.

There was a seagull sitting on the bridge railing next to our minivan, and it looked right at me.

I guess I kind of felt sorry for it, so I tossed a cheese curl out of the sunroof. I have to say, I was pretty impressed when the seagull caught the thing in midair.

I was about to throw it ANOTHER one, but Mom stopped me.

She said seagulls are really aggressive, and giving them "people food" is a bad idea.

She was right about the "aggressive" thing, because two seconds later the seagull was on top of the car, and you could tell it wanted more food.

I threw another one at it to try to make it go away, but the seagull bobbled the cheese curl, which fell right back into the car.

That's when things got BAD.

The seagull hopped down INTO the car and ate the cheese curl off the floor.

For a second, everyone was in a state of shock that a seagull was in our van, and nobody moved a muscle.

The seagull squawked a few times and then tried to fly back out the way it came in. But it missed the opening by about two feet and smacked into the roof.

Then it just went completely nuts, flying around and crashing into the windows. Everyone was in a total panic, and feathers and cheese curls were everywhere.

Then the seagull got greedy and grabbed the bag of cheese curls off the floor. But I snagged it and held on for dear life. Everyone was yelling at me to let go of the bag, but I wasn't giving in.

Finally, the seagull beat me in our tug-of-war and flew straight up through the sunroof, taking the cheese curls with it. But the seagull didn't get far with the bag.

About three-quarters of the cheese curls ended up BACK in the minivan, and from there it was a total nightmare.

A few of the seagulls flew up front, and Rodrick got so freaked out he hit the accelerator. When the birds finally cleared out and things settled down, we had a whole NEW problem to deal with.

Believe it or not, the people in the car that we rear-ended were actually pretty nice.

It was a man and his wife, and they seemed to understand it was an accident. So they exchanged insurance information with Dad, and the police didn't even need to get involved.

If anything GOOD came out of the accident, it was that it got us out of going to the beach.

The BAD news was that now our van wouldn't start, and we had to wait an hour for a tow truck to come.

All the traffic went down to one lane, and that didn't make us too popular with the people trying to cross the bridge.

The guy at the auto-repair shop said we cracked the radiator and it was gonna take at least four or five hours to fix it. That meant we needed to find something to do for the rest of the day.

When we stepped outside, I was pretty shocked to find out we were only two blocks away from Soak Central, which is where I wanted to go in the FIRST place.

I BEGGED Mom to let us go there while we were waiting for the van to get fixed.

She said she would rather we did something "wholesome" like go to a local library, but this time she was outvoted four to one.

So we walked to Soak Central and paid for tickets at the gate. Then we got a locker and put in all the stuff that we didn't want to get wet.

We changed into our bathing suits and met outside the restrooms. It was SUPER crowded, and there was no way we were gonna find five lounge chairs all together. We eventually found ONE chair with a few broken straps, and dumped our towels and the rest of our stuff on it.

Mom and Dad stayed back with Manny, so me and Rodrick were on our own. But Mom said she wanted the two of us to stick together.

We went to the giant wave pool first, but there were about a BILLION people in it.

Rodrick suggested we play hide-and-seek, but, with all the people and rafts in the pool, I knew it would be impossible for the seeker to find the hider.

I said to make it FAIR the hider couldn't swim underwater. I didn't really trust Rodrick not to cheat, but he came up with a way to make sure the hider followed the rules.

Rodrick got a paper place mat from the snack bar and said the hider had to keep it dry to prove he didn't go underwater. And I have to admit I was pretty impressed he came up with that all on his own.

I volunteered to be the first hider and found a spot at the far end of the pool where I knew Rodrick would have trouble finding me.

What I DIDN'T know was that Rodrick had written something on the place mat before giving it to me. Unfortunately, everyone AROUND me noticed before I did.

What he wrote would've been bad enough on its OWN, but the misspelled word somehow made it WORSE.

And even MORE embarrassing was when the lifeguard got down from her chair and told me I had to get out of the pool.

When it comes to Rodrick, I've gotta learn never to trust him. ESPECIALLY at water parks.

I was done with Rodrick after the place-mat thing and didn't care if Mom said we needed to stick together. I left him behind and went to a waterslide by myself.

I hadn't realized how long the line was until I got halfway up the stairs. But by then a ton of people were BEHIND me, and there was no turning back. So I was packed in with these people until I got to the top.

It was really hot, and people were starting to get agitated by how slowly the line was moving.

Then the kid right behind me poked the lady in FRONT of me in the butt with a pool noodle, and she thought it was ME.

So then I had her BOYFRIEND to deal with.

I really didn't want to get into a fight over something like this, but luckily it didn't come to that. We were at the top of the stairs, and it was time to go down the slide.

Unfortunately, the raft was a four-seater, which made things pretty awkward on the ride down.

The slide emptied out into an area where there were a ton of rafts, which was great because it gave me a chance to hide from that woman and her boyfriend. I went round the lazy river twice to make sure I'd lost them.

I'd had enough with the water after that, so I went back to our lounge chair to get my clothes.

But the chair was GONE, and all our stuff was lying in a pile on the ground.

I found the rest of my family at the snack bar getting lunch and told them what happened with our lounge chair.

Mom said it wouldn't be hard to figure out who TOOK it because of the broken straps.

We spread out to look for it, and I searched the area by the wave pool.

Sure enough, our lounge chair was there. But I couldn't BELIEVE who was SITTING in it.

I don't know what the odds are of running into the same people again and again, but this was starting to get RIDICULOUS.

I figured it was best to just let the Beardos HAVE our lounge chair and not make it into a big deal. So, when I caught back up with my family, I pretended I didn't have any luck finding our chair.

By now our food was getting cold, and we still didn't have anywhere to eat. We eventually found a place to sit behind the snack bar.

Everyone seemed ready to leave after that. Mom asked for the key to the locker so she could get our stuff. But I told her I didn't HAVE it.

She said she had given me the key, but I turned both pockets of my bathing suit inside out to prove they were empty.

I was pretty sure she'd given the key to RODRICK, but he said HE didn't have it, either.

Everybody searched themselves for the key, but we all came up empty-handed. This was a HUGE problem, because Mom and Dad's phones and wallets were in that locker, so we couldn't leave until we found it.

We went to an employee at the front counter and told him we lost our key.

But when he asked what our locker number was none of us could remember. There were hundreds of them, and they all looked exactly the same.

He said the locker number was written on the key, but of course THAT information wasn't getting us anywhere.

The guy said the only thing we could do was try to FIND the key, so we split up and retraced our steps across the water park.

Rodrick went to the wave pool where we'd played hide-and-seek, and I went to the lazy river but didn't have any luck.

When we met back up, nobody had found the key. Mom said maybe we accidentally threw it away after we ate, so we dug through the trash near where we sat.

Mom said we should all concentrate real hard and try to remember which locker we put our stuff in and, when I did, I could suddenly see it clearly in my mind.

I told Mom, and we went straight to locker 929. Sure enough, it was locked, and there was no key in the door.

We went back to the guy at the counter to tell him which locker was ours, but we had to wait a long time before we could get his attention.

When we told him our locker number, he got out the master key and walked over to number 929 with us. But by the time we got there the key was back in the slot and the locker was EMPTY.

That meant someone had found our key and STOLEN all our stuff.

Then I thought of ANOTHER possibility: when the Beardos took our lounge chair, they must've taken our KEY, too.

I decided to tell Mom and Dad all about the Beardos and how they probably stole our stuff to get some payback on me. Then I took them to the area where I last saw them sitting.

But when we got there they were GONE.

I was worried they might've already left the park, so I ran to the front gate. And, sure enough, the purple van was pulling away.

I KNEW that family was bad news from the beginning, but I never thought they were capable of THEFT.

Dad used the phone at the front desk to call the police, but the cops said that without a licence-plate number it would be really hard to track down our stolen stuff.

If there was any GOOD news about our situation, it was that the key to the van wasn't in the locker, because it was back at the mechanic's.

So we walked to the auto-repair shop, where the mechanic was getting ready to put in a new radiator. He told Dad it was gonna cost almost three hundred dollars, but Dad told him he couldn't pay because his wallet just got stolen.

Dad told the mechanic he'd mail him a cheque the second we got home, but the guy said he couldn't take an "IOU". He said what he COULD do was put some sealant on the busted radiator, which would last a day or two before it wore off.

But the mechanic said we'd have to run the heater inside the van at full blast to keep the engine from overheating. He said it might sound crazy, but it actually works.

Mom and Dad talked it over and decided we should just drive the van all the way home. We didn't have any money or a phone, but we DID have a full tank of petrol. Dad figured if we drove straight through we'd get back at about 3:00 in the morning.

Mom seemed pretty sad the trip was getting cut short, but, to be honest, I was kind of relieved.

When we got in the van, Dad turned up the heat just like the mechanic told him to, and within about thirty seconds it was a hundred degrees inside the car.

Mom opened all the windows up front, but it was like a FURNACE where I was sitting, since the windows back there don't open.

I told Mom I didn't think I could make it all the way home without dying of heatstroke, but she said I'd be fine as long as I stayed hydrated. Then she got two cases of water out of the boat and brought them into the van.

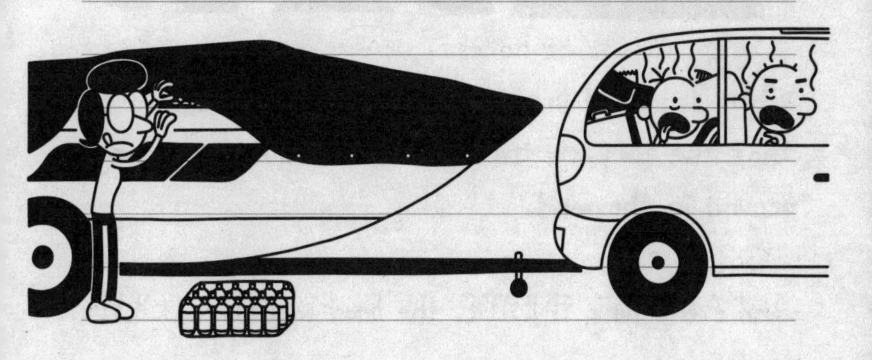

We headed out on to the highway, and I went through four bottles of water in the first hour.

I tried to fall asleep to make the trip go faster, but I got woken up when somebody started honking their horn.

The people in the car next to us were waving their arms and trying to get our attention.

When I looked behind us, I was surprised to see that the tarp on the boat was loose and flapping around in the wind.

And everything INSIDE the boat was flying OUT.

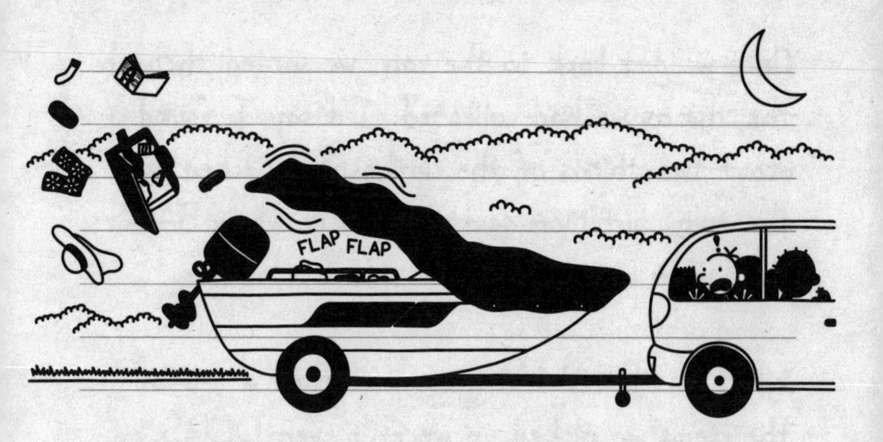

Cars were swerving left and right, trying to avoid our stuff flying through the air. By now, Dad had seen what was going on in the rear-view mirror, and he pulled over to the side of the road.

We spent the next two hours walking down the highway trying to recover all of our stuff. But we had to give up when it got dark.

Once we got back to the van, we sorted through the things we had collected. I'd say I found about two-thirds of the clothes I'd packed for the trip, but Mom said there were whole BAGS that were missing.

What was REALLY gross was that a few of the items we picked up weren't even OURS. Rodrick found a pair of underwear that was as stiff as cardboard.

Once we got back in the car, Mom said we needed to start thinking about eating. Rodrick wanted to open the package of cinnamon rolls that was still in the grocery bag, but Mom said they hadn't been refrigerated and he'd get sick if he ate them.

Mom used the GPS to try to find a place to eat. But the only places that were open at that hour were fast-food restaurants, and Mom wasn't happy about that.

We ended up pulling over at a rest stop along the highway that had a fried chicken place. Since we didn't have any cash or credit cards, we had to scrounge around on the floor of the car for loose change.

We came up with three dollars and fifteen cents, which I was pretty sure wasn't even enough to get a drumstick and a thigh.

Mom said maybe they had a value menu with less expensive items, so we got out of the car and walked to the restaurant.

But, when we got to the entrance, the doors were locked. We could see workers inside, but apparently at that hour the only thing open was the drive-through.

We got back in the car and tried to enter the drive-through lane, but with the boat it was too tight a squeeze. So we had to repark and go through on FOOT.

We stood next to the menu and waited for someone to come on the speaker and take our order, but no one did.

Dad said there must be some kind of sensor that could detect the weight of a car, so we did our best to trigger it.

Eventually, somebody inside noticed us and opened the drive-through window.

Mom asked what we could get with the money we had, and the cashier said we could buy a small box of chicken nuggets and a couple of cookies.

So we got that, plus a handful of barbecue-sauce packets. Then we went back to the van and split the food five ways.

We drove for a half hour or so, but by now it was pretty obvious we weren't gonna make it all the way home in one shot. So we were gonna have to find a place to sleep.

We didn't have any money for a hotel, so Mom tried to find a campsite nearby.

The closest one was ten miles in the opposite direction, though. Dad said we were just gonna have to take the next exit, find a place where we could park and sleep in the car.

I was open to just about anything as long as we could turn the heater off when we stopped.

But, as soon as we took the exit, it was clear we'd made a mistake.

First of all, the road wasn't paved. There weren't any petrol stations or stores or even any houses. There were just trees on either side of the road and no streetlights.

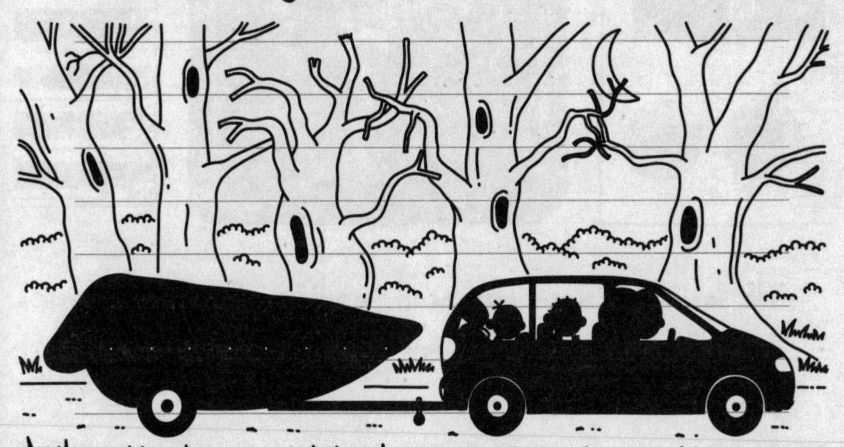

We drove for a long time, but the road was narrow and there wasn't a good place to pull over. I think everyone was getting pretty spooked, and eventually Mom told Dad we should just get back on the highway.

But Dad kept saying he was POSITIVE that at any moment we were gonna find a good place to stop.

The further we went, though, the more nervous Mom became, because now even the GPS didn't know where we were.

We saw some signs up ahead, and we all got excited that maybe we were getting back to civilization. But we were wrong.

Right at the moment when everyone's nerves were totally shot, there was a really loud noise.

Dad swerved off the road, and our car came to a stop in the mud.

My ears were ringing, and I looked around to try to figure out what had happened.

I expected to see broken glass everywhere, but the windows were intact, and there was some kind of weird goo all over them.

Rodrick had the gooey stuff on the back of his head, and he was TOTALLY freaking out.

I still didn't know what was going on, but then I looked in the grocery bag, which had shreds of the cinnamon-roll package inside.

The tube had EXPLODED because the bag was sitting right on top of one of the heater vents.

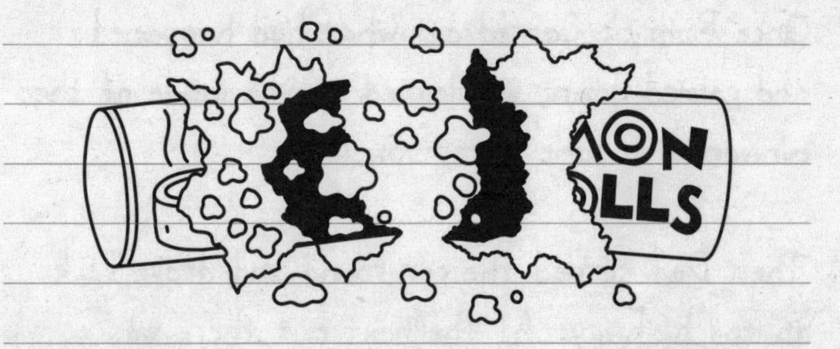

But RODRICK didn't know that yet. He had uncooked cinnamon rolls all over the back of his head, and he thought the dough was his BRAINS.

What upset Rodrick even MORE was when he saw Manny licking the stuff off his fingers.

Once Rodrick figured out what had happened and calmed down, we cleaned up the inside of the minivan with some paper towels.

Then Dad turned the car round and drove back to the highway. At the next exit there was a supermarket with an empty parking lot, so Dad pulled in for the night.

We only had four reclining seats in the van and five people, so Mom volunteered Dad to sleep in the boat.

I know Dad was looking forward to using his boat on this trip, but I'm guessing this was NOT what he had in mind.

Wednesday

It took me a long time to fall asleep last night, and I was woken up at about 6:00 in the morning when the supermarket employees started arriving for work.

By then the sun was up and it was already hot in the car, plus we were all sticky and miserable from sleeping in our clothes.

We walked over to the supermarket to see if they'd let us use the restrooms to wash up, but the manager said the store wouldn't be open to customers for another two hours.

When we were walking back to the car, Mom said we could use Manny's baby wipes to get cleaned up. But then she realized she had accidentally locked the keys inside the minivan.

There was HOPE, though. The sunroof was still open, so Dad tried to FISH the keys out of the cup holder.

After a lot of trying, he still couldn't get the right angle. It looked like we were out of options at that point, but then Mom suggested maybe MANNY could get the keys out.

So Dad lowered Manny through the sunroof by his leash.

Once Manny was in the van, he took his sweet time. First he went to the back and ate the two barbecue-sauce packets we had left. Then he dug through my duffel bag and found a pack of Oreos I'd been saving just in case.

Manny finally made his way to the front of the car and got the keys, but, instead of opening the door to let us in, he started the ENGINE.

Then he fiddled with the knob on the stereo until he found a radio station he liked.

Mom and Dad were pounding on the windows, trying to get Manny to open the door. But then Manny put the car in DRIVE.

I think until then everyone had forgotten that Manny had been trying to run away, because we never would've made the mistake of letting him in the van by himself if we had remembered.

Luckily, Manny wasn't tall enough to reach the accelerator, because, if he could, he would've been long gone.

I think Manny knew his escape plan was foiled, at least for now. Mom finally convinced him to unlock the doors and let us in.

Once we got going again, I started seeing some familiar sights out of the window, because we were basically retracing our path back home.

We were coming up to the town where we'd spent the first night of the trip, and when we passed by the motel we'd stayed in I saw the CRAZIEST thing.

There was a purple van in the parking lot.

I told Dad, and he pulled over. We took a closer look at the van and, sure enough, it was the one that belonged to the Beardos.

That meant they were staying at THIS motel, and were probably using Mom and Dad's credit cards to PAY for it.

We parked our car at the side of the building. Dad said he was gonna call the cops, so he got out to use the phone at the front desk.

But thirty seconds later Dad came running back to the car.

He said he saw the Beardos leaving their room to go down to the pool, and it looked like their door was left open.

Mom said we should stick with the plan and call the police, but Dad said that before we did we should do a little investigation of our OWN.

So we ALL got out and followed Dad to the Beardos' room. Just like he said, the door was open a crack.

Dad nudged it open a little WIDER, and we peeked inside to see if anything of ours was sitting in plain view.

But we couldn't see any of our stuff from where we were standing.

Mom seemed pretty uneasy about what we were doing, but then Dad pushed the door ALL the way open, and there was no turning back.

We couldn't find anything of ours, so if the Beardos DID have any of our stuff they probably carried it with them to the pool.

But as long as we had the run of their room we decided to take full advantage of it. I figured it was OK since we were the ones paying for it.

I think Mom felt we were setting a bad example for Manny, so she took him out to the car.

But the rest of us weren't finished. Me and Rodrick took turns using the bathroom while Dad stood watch at the door.

Then he went in and told us to be lookouts for HIM.

We had pushed our luck, though. The SECOND Dad shut the door to the bathroom, I saw the Beardos coming our way.

Now, I love my dad and all, but I'm too YOUNG to die. So I bolted, and Rodrick was right behind me.

I wasn't there to SEE it, but I'm guessing it was pretty awkward when Mr Beardo opened his bathroom door.

Me and Rodrick got in the van and locked the doors. I was pretty convinced Dad wasn't gonna make it out of the room alive and we were just gonna have to go on without him.

But Mom pulled the car round to the front of the motel, and when she did Dad burst out of the Beardos' room.

Somehow Dad had got the idea to grab their car keys on his way out.

Before he got in our car he chucked the keys into some bushes, which bought us some time.

I think we must've gone two miles down the road before Dad even bothered to pull his trousers back up.

We high-fived each other because we had escaped with our lives. But, in our rush to get away, we forgot to turn on the HEATER.

And a few seconds later the RADIATOR conked out.

Mom had to cut across two lanes of traffic to get the van into the breakdown lane. But in the spot where we pulled over there was a broken bottle, and we rolled right over it.

We got out of the car so we could change the tyre. Dad opened the back hatch to find his jack, but unfortunately I had taken it out before we left for the trip to make room for my PILLOW.

The only thing we could do at that point was wait for help to come.

Eventually, a car pulled over behind us, but when it got closer I knew we were in big trouble.

It was a purple van.

I figured the Beardos might try to ram us with their car, so I braced for impact. But the van slowed down, and when the doors opened it wasn't the Beardos at ALL.

It was pretty obvious that whoever these guys were they were here to HELP.

But they didn't speak English, so we were having trouble communicating with them. Mom and Dad tried to act out what was wrong with the car, and I'm sure the two guys thought my parents had completely lost their minds.

Then Manny surprised EVERYONE by speaking in perfect Spanish.

The conversation between Manny and the two guys lasted a long time, so I figured Manny was explaining everything that had happened on our trip.

He must've done a good job making the guys feel sorry for us, because, the next thing you knew, they were offering us a RIDE. And I'm happy to say their air-conditioning worked GREAT.

I think we assumed these guys were taking us to a mechanic or something, but we were wrong.

We should've realized that if MANNY was the one doing all the talking we'd end up going where HE wanted to go.

Sunday

Like I said before, Mom was right about pigs being smart. She had it house-trained within a week, and the pig even knows a few tricks already.

My only real complaint is that now I never get a chance to watch my shows on TV, because the pig has figured out how to use the remote.

But I'm gonna let that go, because I don't want to get bitten a second time.

It's taken a while for everything to get back to normal after the trip. Dad had to take a few more days off work to cancel all his credit cards and get new ones.

And tomorrow Mom and Dad are supposed to go out and get new drivers' licences and phones.

Our minivan's been at the mechanic's since it was towed. We gave the BOAT to the drivers who helped us out as a way of saying thanks, which was actually Mom's suggestion.

Mom's been saying that, even though our trip didn't go the way we planned, it was still an adventure. She's been working on an article to send in to "Family Frolic" that I seriously hope does NOT get published.

Mom's also been making a scrapbook, and she asked everyone to contribute a souvenir to put inside.

I was going through the clothes I wore on the trip, and when I picked up my shorts something small fell out on to the floor.

It was the KEY from Soak Central.

I couldn't believe I had the key all along. It turns out I was wrong about the locker number. But I should get SOME credit for being CLOSE.

Now that I have the key, I have a tough decision to make. It feels like a page from one of those Choose Your Own Adventure books.

I figure I have three basic choices. One, I can tell Mom and Dad the truth and deal with the consequences. Two, I can plant the key in RODRICK'S dirty laundry and let HIM take the blame. Or, three, I can flush the key down the toilet and forget this whole thing ever happened.

There's a fourth option that involves the pig, but I haven't worked out the details of THAT one yet.

But like I said before, whenever I have a difficult choice to make, I always seem to pick the wrong one. And, whichever way I go here, it's hard to see this story having a happy ending.

ACKNOWLEDGMENTS

Thanks to my wonderful family for your continued love, support and encouragement.

Thanks to everyone at Abrams for treating every Wimpy Kid book like it's the first. Thanks especially to Charlie Kochman, Michael Jacobs, Jason Wells, Veronica Wasserman, Steve Tager, Susan Van Metre, Jen Graham, Chad W. Beckerman, Alison Gervais, Elisa Garcia, Erica La Sala and Scott Auerbach.

Thanks to all my international publishers for bringing Greg's stories to kids all over the world. I feel very grateful for the friendships I've made over the past few years.

Thanks to Shaelyn Germain and Anna Cesary for everything you do to keep all the balls in the air at the same time.

Thanks to Paul Sennott and Ike Williams for all the great advice.

Thanks to everyone in Hollywood who has worked to bring Greg Heffley to life on the big and small screens. Thanks especially to Sylvie Rabineau, Keith Fleer, Nina Jacobson, Brad Simpson, Ralph Milero, Roland Poindexter, Elizabeth Gabler and Vanessa Morrison.

Thanks to everyone at Poptropica, especially Jess Brallier.

ABOUT THE AUTHOR

Jeff Kinney is a #1 *New York Times* bestselling author and a five-time Nickelodeon Kids' Choice Award winner for Favourite Book. Jeff has been named one of *Time* magazine's 100 Most Influential People in the World. He is also the creator of Poptropica, which was named one of *Time* magazine's 50 Best Websites. He spent his childhood in the Washington, D.C., area and moved to New England in 1995. Jeff lives with his wife and two sons in Massachusetts, where they own a bookstore, An Unlikely Story.

Feeling sneaky?
Check out this
EXCLUSIVE EXTRACT
from
DIARY of a Wimpy Kid
OLD SCHOOL
Jeff Kinney

SEPTEMBER

Saturday

Grown-ups are always talking about the "good old days" and how things were so much better when THEY were kids.

But I think they're just jealous because MY generation has all this fancy technology and stuff they didn't have growing up.

Believe me, I'm sure when I have kids of my own I'm gonna be the exact same way my parents are NOW.

Mom's always saying that when SHE was younger it was great because everybody in town knew everybody else and it was like one giant family.

But that doesn't sound so great to ME. I like my privacy, and I really don't need everyone knowing my personal business.

Mom says the problem with society these days is that everybody's got their nose in a screen and nobody takes the time to get to know the people who live around them.

I don't really see eye to eye with Mom on that issue, though.

Personally, I think a little separation is a GOOD thing.

Lately, Mom's been going around town with a petition to get people to stop using their phones and electronic gadgets for forty-eight hours.

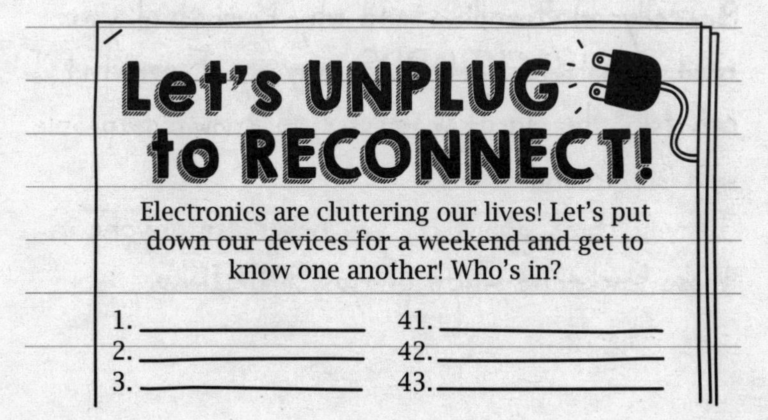

Let's UNPLUG to RECONNECT!

Electronics are cluttering our lives! Let's put down our devices for a weekend and get to know one another! Who's in?

1. ______________ 41. ______________
2. ______________ 42. ______________
3. ______________ 43. ______________

Mom needs a hundred signatures before she can take the petition to the town hall, but she's having trouble getting people to put their names on it.

I'm just hoping she gives up on this idea soon, because it's kind of exhausting for the rest of us to pretend we don't know her.

I really don't understand why Mom thinks we need to go BACKWARDS, anyway. From what I can tell, the old days weren't that much fun.

If you think about it, you never see anyone in those black-and-white photos SMILING.

In the old days, people were just a whole lot TOUGHER than they are today.

But human beings have EVOLVED, and now we need things like electric toothbrushes and shopping malls and soft-serve ice cream to survive.

I bet our ancestors would be pretty disappointed with the way we turned out. But once somebody invented air-conditioning there really was no turning back.

We've got so spoiled that pretty soon we won't even have to leave our homes if we don't want to.

In fact, the way we're headed, I'll bet a thousand years from now human beings won't even have SPINES.

Some people complain that all this technology has made us soft. But, if you ask me, that's not necessarily a BAD thing.

There are all SORTS of luxuries nowadays that make people's lives better. Take baby wipes, for example. People were using regular toilet paper for hundreds of years, and then all of a sudden some genius came up with an idea that was a total game changer.

What really amazes me is that it took so LONG for people to come up with the idea. I seriously can't believe the guy who invented the light bulb didn't see baby wipes coming.

And who KNOWS what crazy thing someone's gonna come up with next to make our lives easier. Whatever it is, though, I'll be the first in line to buy it.

But if Mom had HER way we'd be living like people did before there were computers and phones and baby wipes.

And I really don't want to imagine living in a world without baby wipes.

- **Meet** Jeff Kinney
- Relive **favourite moments**
- Learn **how to draw** the cartoons
- Watch **cool movie clips**
- Discover **top writing tips**
- Find **awesome trailers**

And look out for lots of extra surprises from Greg, Rowley, Fregley and more . . .

ZOO-WEE MAMA
Get sketching!
Wimpy Kid
SKETCHBOOK!
Wimpy Kid
SKETCHBOOK!
Two in one. Draw and write!
THE Wimpy Kid
SCHOOL PLANNER
THIS AMAZING PIECE OF TECHNOLOGY WILL HELP YOU
KEEP TRACK OF HOMEWORK ASSIGNMENTS
MANAGE YOUR TIME
STAY ORGANIZED
PLAN YOUR SOCIAL LIFE
AND POSSIBLY GIVE YOU X-RAY VISION*
COMES FULLY CHARGED AND READY TO USE
Everything you'll need to survive middle school

MORE Wimpy Kid STUFF!

From journals to calendars, notebooks and more, check it all out at

www.wimpykidclub.co.uk

WANT MORE
Wimpy Kid?
Go to
www.wimpykidclub.co.uk/audio
to listen to extracts from the
Wimpy Kid audio series.
Available on CD and digital download.